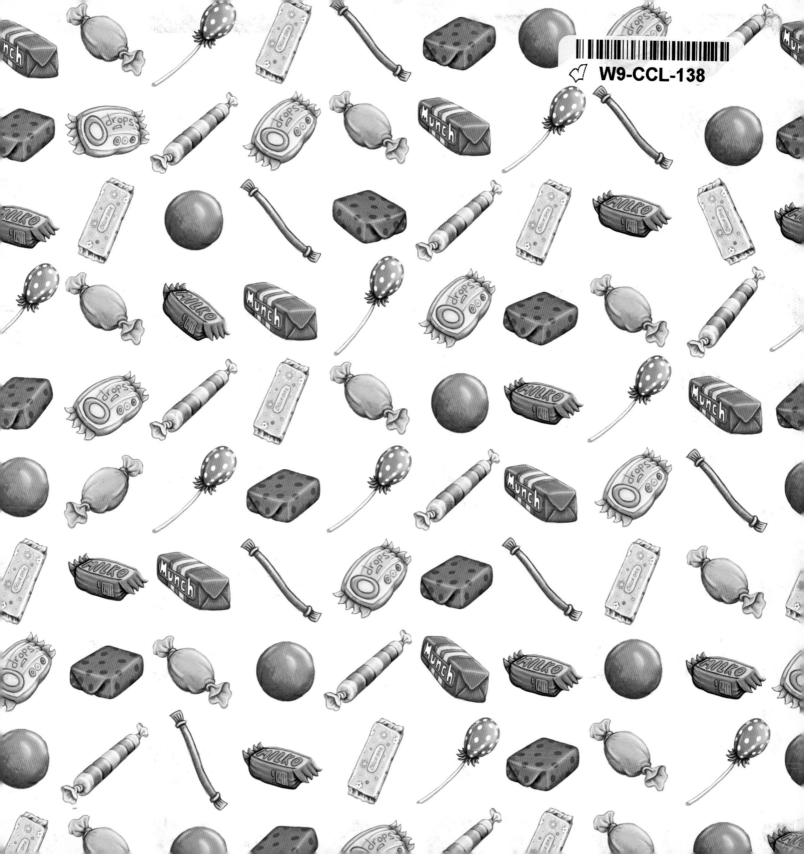

For Margot and Jerry

Balzer + Bray is an imprint of HarperCollins Publishers.
Otter Loves Halloween!
Copyright © 2015 by Sam Garton
All rights reserved. Manufactured in China.
No part of this book may be used or reproduced in any manner whatsoever without written permission except in the case of brief quotations embodied in critical articles and reviews. For information address HarperCollins Children's Books, a division of HarperCollins Publishers, 195 Broadway, New York, NY 10007. www.harpercollinschildrens.com

ISBN 978-0-06-236666-5

The artist used Adobe Photoshop to create the digital illustrations for this book.
Typography by Dana Fritts
15 16 17 18 19   SCP   10 9 8 7 6 5 4 3 2 1
❖
First Edition

OTTER
Loves Halloween!

SAM GARTON

BALZER + BRAY

An Imprint of HarperCollins*Publishers*

Halloween is the best holiday ever!
Teddy and I had been waiting a very long time for Halloween.
There were lots of things we had to do to get ready.

First, Otter Keeper took us pumpkin shopping.

But Otter Keeper is not very good
at choosing pumpkins.

Teddy and I found the right one eventually.
It was very big, so we had to promise we'd
help carry it back.

When we got home, Otter Keeper ran into a few problems carving our pumpkin.

I told Giraffe to help, because Teddy and I had to start decorating the house.

We did decorate a few things we shouldn't have, but overall we did a great job.

Finally, I had to organize everyone's Halloween
costumes. I dressed up as a superscary witch!

I couldn't get my magical broomstick to work,
but I looked really scary, so that didn't matter.

Teddy decided to dress up as a scary mummy.
We both agreed he looked almost as scary as I did!

Giraffe wanted to dress up for Halloween too,
but I wasn't sure about his costume idea.

Otter Keeper said you can dress up as whatever
you want on Halloween.

So Giraffe was a fairy.

He wasn't really taking Halloween seriously.
Everyone knows fairies aren't scary.

So I added some teeth.

We spent the rest of the afternoon practicing with our costumes by scaring Pig.

Teddy and I were very good at this.

Giraffe was not. But it was his fault for dressing as an unscary fairy.

Finally the doorbell rang! The trick-or-treaters
were here at last!

Ding
dong!

It was then that we ran into a problem.

The trick-or-treaters were very scary—almost too scary!

I suddenly remembered I had lots
of important things to do under
the bed upstairs.

I took Pig with me too. He was
really scared.

I was worried Halloween had been ruined.
But then Otter Keeper had a little chat with us.

We both felt a lot better.

Then Otter Keeper had a clever idea.
I was even allowed to help!

Ding dong!

When the next trick-or-treaters arrived,
we were ready for them.

Our new costumes worked perfectly. These trick-or-treaters sounded even scarier than the ones before. But things are much less scary when you can't really see them.

This was definitely the best Halloween ever!

Until the trick-or-treaters stopped coming.

Otter Keeper told me they all had gone home,
because it was almost bedtime.

But I wasn't tired at all!

So I made special costumes for everyone.

It's a good thing we finished when we did. . . .

It was way past Pig's bedtime.

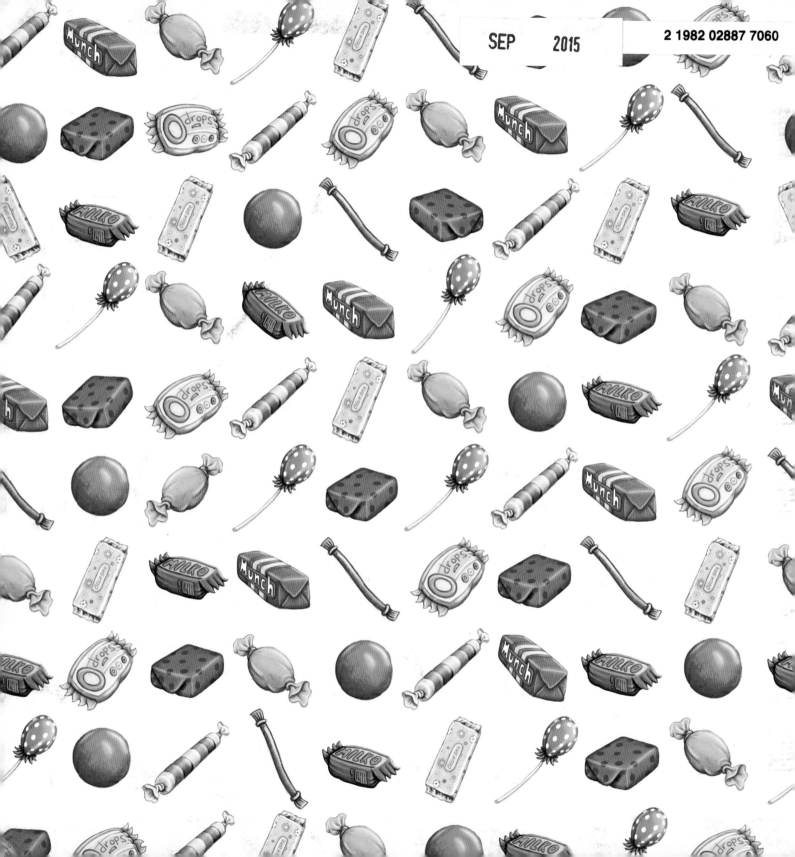